STREET HEROES

For my brothers - Steve, Sim and Jake

First published in Great Britain and the USA in 2010 by
Frances Lincoln Children's Books, 4 Torriano Mews,
Torriano Avenue, London NW5 2RZ
www.franceslincoln.com

A catalogue record for this book is available from the British Library.

ISBN 978-1-84780-077-0

Set in Bembo

Printed in Croydon, Surrey, UK by CPI Bookmarque in February 2010

1 3 5 7 9 8 6 4 2

STREET HEROES

JOE LAYBURN

F

FRANCES LINCOLN
CHILDREN'S BOOKS

GEORGIE

You know my dad. You've seen him on television, or on those massive posters, or even in the flesh. So you'll understand why I could never be friends with someone who was black, or Asian, or different, in any way, from what I am - proper white British. That's what I thought, until I started hearing voices.

It was at one of Dad's rallies. There was a big crowd. There always was when he went to places like Barking, where lots of white people live on run-down estates.

Brian, one of Dad's bodyguards, was getting twitchy, not so anyone else would have noticed, but I did. He was sweating, and he kept rubbing the back of his pockmarked neck. He had this thing stuck in his ear that meant he could hear what Tony and Mart were saying. The three of them, all built like heavyweight boxers, were not supposed to carry guns, but I imagined they did on days like this. They were always ready for trouble.

Some people loved my Dad. I know for a fact that Brian, Tony and Mart would have taken a bullet for him if they'd had to. But many people loathed him. And that's because, as the do-gooders claimed, my Dad 'spread racial hatred'.

When we first arrived at the Barking rally, a pale, skinny, blonde woman had leant in through the window of our car and shouted at Dad, "You're a scumbag, Smith! My great-grandad died in the war trying to stop Nazis like you." The press were there, their cameras clicking, so Dad just smiled back at her. "Nice to meet you too, darling."

Whenever he was about to speak to a

crowd, Dad looked like a preacher. His eyes shone and he glowed with a kind of religious excitement. He was wearing a dark suit, a white shirt with an electric blue tie, and the cufflinks my sister Albion had given him for his birthday. They had this Union Jack design and he kept fidgeting with them, which told me he was nervous too. Dad didn't have a speech written down. Once he started, words just seemed to fly from his mouth like birds released from a cage. He stepped towards the microphone at the front of the platform and stretched out his arms for the crowd to be silent. Then he turned back to me and winked. I grinned at him and gave him the thumbs up.

"You all right?" he shouted, his voice hoarse and gravelly as always. It echoed round the town centre, bouncing off the shop windows and office buildings. "I said, are you all right?" This time the crowd called back that they were.

He paused for a beat or two, then shook

his head, as if he couldn't quite believe what he'd just heard.

"Well, when I look around this place, I'm surprised you say that. Don't get me wrong, I'm happy if you're happy. But to my mind, the people of Barking, the real people of Barking, deserve better than this. You deserve better than to have the refugees and the asylum-seekers and the illegals taking what's rightfully yours. If that's not a problem for you, then I made a mistake coming here. But if that's something that worries you like it worries me, well, then I'm glad I came to speak to you today. In your hearts, people of Barking, don't you think you deserve a lot more than you're getting? Cos I reckon you're being cheated out of your birthright. Am I right, or what?"

He cupped a hand to his right ear and this time they roared back at him like an incoming tide. I looked out at the white faces, raised arms waving little flags like you'd see on sandcastles at Southend or Clacton. And then the chanting started, like a rough sea beating against rocks:

"Smiffy, Smiffy…" My dad, George Smith Senior glanced back again to where I was standing.

"Hear that, Georgie boy? These are our people."

I started to smile but suddenly my head seemed to fill with a nuclear-size explosion, my body went rigid and the can of fizzy drink I'd been holding slipped through my fingers. It clattered down the side of the platform, but that noise was all but drowned out by what felt like wave upon wave of radio interference crashing around inside my skull. My mind was spinning wildly and when it finally stopped, someone else seemed to have grabbed control of it. A girl's voice was speaking inside my head.

My name is Fatima. I know that you can hear me. Please don't be afraid.

My vision had become distorted like a TV set on the blink, and I could feel myself swaying from side to side. Then Brian's arm was around me, holding me up. Clearly he thought I was about to faint. I squinted hard and my dad's anxious face swam slowly into view.

I say anxious, but he looked annoyed too.

"What's the matter with you, Georgie?" he hissed.

"I thought I heard this girl's voice inside my head. She said her name was Fatima."

"Fatima?" he growled. "You're having a laugh."

OMAR

My brother Sadiq used to be a lot of fun. He's six years older than me, but he never pushed me around or anything. He was always religious. I am too. But then he got really political, and that's when things started to go wrong.

Our father always said that we should let other people get on with their lives and trust they'd leave us to get on with ours. I suppose that made sense to me. But Sadiq would snap back at him: "What if they won't leave us alone? What if they don't approve of us? What then?"

There was a group of young men at his university who distributed leaflets full of anger at the governments of Britain and America and the way they treat Muslims. One time the police tried to move them on when they were handing out their leaflets on Green Street, up from West Ham football ground. Sadiq got really mad. "What gives you the right to stop our free speech?" he asked the police officers who had pulled up in their van and piled out onto the street. "Shouldn't you be down the road there, stopping the football hooligans from fighting each other?"

"We've had some complaints about you, fella. You're causing an obstruction and I can see your mouth is going to get you in bother."

I was with him that day but I knew there was little point trying to stop him back-chatting the policeman.

"I don't recognise your authority over me," Sadiq muttered.

The policeman heard him.

"You'll recognise my boot up your backside,

if you don't stop giving me lip, sunshine."

The other policemen laughed, which made Sadiq even more furious.

"You'll have to arrest me, because I'm not prepared to move from this spot," he said.

"Is that right?"

"It's not right that you're persecuting me. That isn't right at all." Sadiq pulled at his beard nervously.

"Please, Sadiq," I said, grabbing a fistful of his white robe and trying to drag him away. "Let's just go."

"Who's this, then?" asked another of the policeman. He was from the North somewhere, with an accent that sounded like Bradford or Leeds.

Sadiq just shook his head.

"I'm his little brother," I said. "We don't want any trouble, officer.

Sadiq glared at me as if I was cosying up to the enemy.

"Seems to me that your kind are always looking for trouble," the policeman said.

"That's not true," I started to protest, but suddenly the voice of my sister Fatima was in my head, calm and soothing.

Leave it be, Omar. If Sadiq wants to talk his way into Forest Gate police station, then let him. You need to come home.

Fatima had always been able to do this: get inside my head, read my mind, share her thoughts with me, even when we were miles apart. It felt normal to me, but I knew I had to keep it a secret. A lot of people hate it if you're different from them.

MELISSA

The first time I heard Fatima's voice, I was alone, as usual, in the playground of Collinson Primary School. There was a group of girls in Year 6 and they decided who was in the in-crowd and who wasn't. They seemed to change their minds every day, which kept those girls on the edge of the group almost sick with worry. For me, it never changed, though. The popular girls didn't consider me at all.

I'd been spending lunchtime with Mrs Stott, the new playground assistant, following her like a big dog around the rectangle of worn grass that ran alongside the netball courts.

"Melissa, do you want to try sitting on the buddy bench? Then people will know that you're looking to make friends."

I glanced at the bench. Next to it was a sign like you see at bus-stops that said, 'Wait here for buddies!'

"There's no point. No one wants to play with me."

"It'd be worth a try, wouldn't it?" She pulled back the sleeve of her red woollen coat and squinted at her watch. "Lunch break won't be over for another twenty minutes or so."

"I'm all right on my own. I've got used to it."

Mrs Stott had almost white-blond hair with black roots that were showing through.

"Are you going to keep your hair blonde or let it go back to its natural colour?" I asked her.

Her mouth twitched into a half-smile.

"That's a funny sort of question, Melissa."

"I was just aksing, yeah. Trying to make conversation with you."

Mrs Stott laughed. "Fair enough, then. I've been meaning to do something with it. I just haven't had the time."

"I think you should let it go black again. At the moment it looks a bit like you don't care about your appearance. It's a bit, you know, cheap."

Mrs Stott's smile disappeared like a cloud had passed across her usually sunny face.

"That's not a very nice thing to say."

"I'm just being honest. Innit people say that honesty is the best policy?"

"Go and sit on the buddy bench, there's a good girl."

I walked slowly past the bench and sat down under a leafless tree that grew next to the fence. Kele, this tall Nigerian kid, walked past bouncing a bright orange basketball. He made a clicking sound with his mouth.

"What are you looking at?" I asked him.

"Something fat and annoying," he muttered.

"I hate you, Kele," I shouted after him.

13

"I hate all of you!"

That's the exact moment when I got my first Fatima thunderbolt. After a while, it doesn't hurt any more when she talks to you. But when you're not used to it, it's like a police siren going off inside your head. If I hadn't been sitting down already, I swear I'd have fallen over.

GEORGIE

At school on Monday morning, people were huddled together in exclusive little groups, whispering and glancing in my direction. That made it just another day at Caddogan Hall. I'd never liked the place but I could see why it impressed people when they first saw it, my dad included. It was a rambling, grey building, with turrets everywhere, which loomed up dramatically out of the flat, boring Hertfordshire countryside. A high wall surrounded it – to keep out the peasants, according to my best and only mates Mark and Scooter. Like me, they were 'day pupils' who lived within driving distance, but a lot of kids boarded, which meant Caddogan Hall was basically their home.

I would have felt sorry for the boarders if I'd liked any of them, but I kept away. Quite a few were foreign, from places like Hong Kong and Malaysia. I couldn't see that we'd have much in common. The boys all seemed to like Maths and chess and stuff like that, things I was no good at. One of the Chinese ones who used the English name Fred and played on the rugby team had made an effort to be friendly. But he soon backed off when someone explained to him about my background. I didn't care. Dad only wanted me to socialise with my "own kind". That, he said, was the main reason he was prepared to pay for private education. Not that he'd been able to keep me away entirely from the "foreigners and ethnics" he spent his life moaning about.

Mark and Scooter were late as usual, so I threw my rucksack down on the flagstones just inside the heavy iron front gates and pretended to be interested in the timetable on the back of my planner.

You know that sixth sense you get when someone's approaching you? I glanced up and, sure enough, one of the prefects was striding towards me with a smug smile creasing his pudding face.

"Morning, Smith. I've been looking for you."

"Is that right?"

"I'm delighted to say you're in a whole world of trouble. It's only a matter of time till the school gets rid of you. Everyone knows you're a racist and a thug, just like your father."

"My dad doesn't have a problem paying the fees, and Caddogan Hall seems happy enough to take our money, so I reckon I'll be staying for a while yet."

Dawkins, or Dawson, or whatever his name was, rocked back on his well-polished shoes and puffed himself up to his full height of about five foot three.

"Seriously, aren't you embarrassed having George Smith as your dad? He's a common little man with some nasty ideas."

"So what exactly do you object to? His ideas, or the fact that he's common?"

He didn't answer, so I picked up my rucksack of books and pushed past him. He called after me.

"Erm, I have a message from Mr Atkinson. He wants to see you in his study at first break. It's about you and Adam Rosen, in case you were wondering."

"I know what it's about," I said.

Mr Atkinson's study was like a well-furnished hobbit-hole. Light beams hardly dared to penetrate it, wood panelling of the darkest kind lined the walls, and there were shelves of dusty old books that appeared not to have been taken down and opened in my lifetime. The room smelled musty, which may have been due to the books, or to Mr Atkinson himself, who always wore a brown suit spattered with gravy and other unidentifiable substances from the Caddogan Hall kitchens. Wiry grey hair sprouted from his head, and out of his ears and nostrils. Pretty much everything about my housemaster's appearance was off-putting, and yet Mr Atkinson was widely liked because he was felt to be fair. Scruffy and disorganised, but always fair.

"Sit," he said, when I entered. He motioned to an antique wooden chair, on which was placed a teetering pile of pale blue exercise books. I moved them onto the threadbare rug and sat down. The legs of the chair wobbled worryingly underneath me.

Caddogan Hall was a no-smoking environment and the pipe that Mr Atkinson held clamped between his yellowed teeth was unlit. Still, the room smelled as though someone had recently been having a smoke. I waited. And waited. Finally, Mr Atkinson put down the fountain pen he'd been using to scratch out a lengthy letter and fixed me with his watery blue eyes.

"It's about Adam Rosen," he said.

"I know, sir. The thing is, sir, Rosen hates me."

Mr Atkinson raised one of his bushy grey eyebrows.

"He certainly hates what he thinks you stand for. What *do* you stand for, Smith?"

Trust me, it wasn't the first time I'd had a conversation like this at Caddogan Hall. Pretty much everyone assumed that my view of the world was the same as my dad's.

"I'm not sure what I stand for. If you mean, am I proud to be British, I suppose I am. My dad's always telling me I should be. Do I have a problem with people who aren't white, or with Jews like Rosen? I suppose I do, because they all seem to have a problem with me."

"So you're a victim?"

"I didn't say that."

"But you feel it."

"Look, sir, I'm thirteen years old. I'm starting to feel like I don't think the same way my dad does on every single issue, but everyone assumes I do, so I might as well."

"So, in time, you might be prepared to rub

along with people of different backgrounds. You might even become friends with some of them."

I jutted my jaw out at Mr Atkinson.

"I didn't say that either. If they leave me alone, I'll leave them alone."

Mr Atkinson sipped from a chipped enamel mug that had been perching precariously on top of an opened dictionary. He grimaced.

"I'm always doing that," he explained, "leaving hot drinks till they get too cold."

He wiped his mouth with his sleeve. Then he remembered what we were there to talk about.

"Rosen tells me he doesn't want to make an issue of what happened, but I can't ignore the fact that he's sporting a rather impressive black eye."

"Did he accuse me of calling him names – you know, racist stuff?"

"No, he didn't. He actually admitted that he'd been badgering you, trying to get you to distance yourself from your father. I think he said he'd demanded that you 'denounce' your father, which is quite a word, and quite an idea, isn't it?"

"I told him if he kept going on about my dad, I'd hit him. So I did."

"So you did. . ."

I stared hard at Mr Atkinson, at his wild hair and bulbous nose.

"Are you going to expel me, sir?"

He laughed.

"Expel you? Absolutely not. You'll be getting a Saturday detention, but my plan, Smith, is to integrate you – to force you to fit in, whatever that takes. The first thing you're going to do is apologise to Rosen. And you're going to shake his hand."

I was supposed to go straight to the classroom where Adam Rosen was doing Latin or Greek or something and ask if he could be excused to speak to me for a few minutes. I tapped on the door of Room A12, coughed and entered. Three rows of pupils were bent over their desks working on some kind of test. Their teacher,

Mr Stokes, was clicking idly on a computer mouse and checking the value of his stocks and shares. I could see this, as could anyone else who cared to look, because his computer was linked to the interactive whiteboard, which glowed like a cinema screen behind him.

"Ah, it's our resident Blackshirt. How are you today, young Mosley? I mean, Smith."

Mr Stokes had a running joke about me and Sir Oswald Mosley, whose British Union of Fascists had worn uniforms in the 1930s, just like the notorious Italian Blackshirts and Adolf Hitler's SS.

"Sir, Mr Atkinson has asked you several times to stop making comments about Oswald Mosley when you see me."

Mr Stokes took his hand away from the mouse and placed it theatrically at the side of his head.

"Has he really? Mr Atkinson, you say? I must have missed that particular memo. Fair enough, Smith, no more mention of storm-troopers smashing up Jewish shops. No more references to those ever-so-stylish black shirts. Consider me reprimanded, dear boy. It stops right here."

I looked down at my shoes. I would have loved to use them to kick him until he really did shut up.

"Sir, I'm here to ask if I could have a word with Rosen outside in the corridor."

"You want Rosen, you say. By God, Rosen, he has come for the Jews after all. Are you sure you want to step outside with him?"

The class had all put their pens down now and were laughing, Rosen included.

"I think I'll be OK, sir," he said.

"Well if you're sure, Rosen. If you really are sure, off you go. But watch him. We don't want him blacking your other eye, do we?"

Mr Stokes stared hard at me and now there was not a flicker of amusement on his face.

"Smith, Mr Rosen is one of my most dedicated pupils. He's not used to your rough stuff. You can step outside for your little chat if you wish, but leave the door open so I'll hear if he starts screaming."

Adam Rosen pulled the door almost shut behind him and stood before me squinting. His left eye was half closed, the skin around it purple and orange. Mr Atkinson must have talked things through with him, because he seemed to be ready for my apology. But now that we were facing each other, I found the words sticking in my throat. Rosen had provoked me. He'd kept jibing at me long after I'd warned him what was going to happen. I was pretty sure my dad wouldn't have wanted me to be shaking his hand. Most probably, Dad would have been proud of what I'd done.

I started to turn away from him, but suddenly I felt this pain flash around inside my head like an electric eel burrowing deep into my brain and shorting all the circuits. I staggered forward and Rosen, who looked suddenly terrified, stepped aside, bullfighter-like. I slid down the smooth green wall of the corridor and crashed to the floor. I could feel myself writhing and twitching like a fish that's found itself on the deck of a trawler, but it all seemed as if it was happening to someone else. I'd seen one of the sixth-formers having an epileptic fit in the swimming pool. Maybe I was experiencing something similar. But then I heard that voice again – the girl's voice I'd heard at the rally. That's when I decided I was simply going round the twist.

Please, you must make things right with this boy.

I stared up at Rosen, whose head seemed to be floating up near the ceiling like a balloon. He'd been joined by a perplexed-looking Mr Stokes, who bobbed along beside him.

"Crikey, Rosen," I heard him say. "Did you do this?"

That's when I shut down completely. Apparently, they had to carry me – unconscious – to the medical room.

MELISSA

From the start, Fatima told me I had to be more "diplomatic" with people – by which she meant that I shouldn't just blurt out the first thing that came into my head. That was hard. My brain seems to be wired differently from everyone else's. My teacher, Miss de Souza, said I was "blunt, borderline-rude" and that it was something I had to work on with my learning support assistant, Stacey.

Stacey thought my moods might improve if I stopped eating so much junk food, especially between meals. But that was hard too, and easy enough for her to say. She stayed skinny and pretty whatever she ate. By the age of nine, I was taller than all the other kids in my year and fatter than everyone else in the school, apart from Jamal who ended up in Newham General Hospital because of his weight issues.

Fatima said I was one of her projects. She said she liked talking to people whose minds she could change. It was a challenge for her. She wanted to make the world a better place and she was starting from the bottom up – which meant, I suppose, people like me.

Having Fatima's voice inside my head was like having a friend, only better in some ways because I didn't have to explain things to her. It's like my brain was a computer and she had access to all the important files. What I'm saying is, she knew what I was thinking and I couldn't hide stuff from her.

I remember one time getting upset because I wanted her to speak only to me, like we were best friends, and not talk to anyone else. But she said it couldn't be that way. Fatima spoke to lots of other children. She said one day we might all be able to meet up – when the time was right.

After she'd gone, I used to feel really empty and wish that I could contact her. Fatima said that if I kept concentrating, I might be able to send my thoughts in her direction rather than just waiting for her to contact me. But that never happened. When I asked her if some of the other children could start conversations with her in their heads, she said lots of them could, but most couldn't. When I asked if we could meet up some time soon, she said that wouldn't be possible for now.

I knew she wasn't far away and it made me angry that I couldn't just go round her house and meet her face to face. She told me to be patient.

I tried to keep Fatima a secret, but I remember one time when I really slipped up. I was outside the classroom with Stacey cleaning the paint trays. I'd been difficult all morning and I'd made Stacey cry, which wasn't that hard because she was too soft to work with me really. I'd told her I hated her and only pretended to like her. That's when Fatima's voice popped into my head, all soothing and sweet, telling me to be nice.

"Be nice? Be nice to that cow?" I wasn't really thinking straight and I actually shouted the words out loud, which made Stacey go all wide-eyed and scared. She started backing away from me as I carried on this noisy conversation with someone who wasn't even there. "You must be joking, Fatima," I cried. "She thinks I'm nothing and she's so special."

With that, I pulled the paintbrushes out of the jam jar and threw the dirty water all over poor, frightened Stacey. She was wearing this white top with 'D&G' on it in sparkly silver letters. It was probably a knock-off, but she was all pleased with it because she'd got it from her boyfriend, Reece. Now it was soaked in watery brown muck and Stacey started howling. Miss de Souza rushed out into the hall and Mr Hammond came from next door, both of them shouting as if there was some kind of emergency. An hour later they'd got the

educational psychologist out to talk to me, but by then I'd stopped feeling even the slightest bit angry. The problem was, I couldn't stop giggling, which made everyone else even more upset.

I think of those days as "the bad days" because now I'm a whole lot better. But the wonderful thing about Fatima is that she always liked me, whatever I did. And I did do some terrible things.

OMAR

If Fatima, our sister, had been able to read my brother's mind, or talk to him like she talked to me, life would have been much simpler. I knew she was concerned that Sadiq had stopped going to our mosque and was mixing with these dodgy extremists. She'd asked me to keep a close eye on him, which was difficult in some ways because he was never around, and easy in others because we shared a bedroom and I could root around in his personal stuff without much risk of getting caught.

My side of the room was a mess, like a

clothes bomb had gone off in the corner. There were empty Lucozade Sports bottles and sweet wrappers under my bed, and socks and pants and things all over the floor. Until recently, Sadiq had been just as bad, but now he was much tidier. He'd taken down his football posters and thrown out most of his clothes. He actually made his bed in the morning before he caught the bus to uni.

It was after he'd left one morning that I saw something sticking out from under his mattress. It looked like the corner of a magazine but when I pulled it out, I realised it was a scrapbook. Sadiq hadn't written anything on the cover to show what was inside and for a second I thought about just shoving it back and going down for my breakfast. I wasn't sure I wanted any concrete evidence of what my big brother was getting up to.

Finally, I did open it and discovered it was full of newspaper cuttings. There was a picture of a man I recognised as the Fascist politician George Smith under a headline which read,

"Big gains for the far right". As I turned the pages I realised that all the clippings were about him. There were profiles about his background and his wife and children too. Smith was always trying to make out that he was a reasonable sort of man, but Sadiq had scribbled all over the cuttings things like "lies" and "disgrace" in angry red pen.

I was so absorbed in what I was reading that I didn't take in the sound of footsteps coming up the stairs or the door handle turning. When I looked up from the scrapbook, Sadiq was in front of me. It was raining outside and his clothes were soaked.

"What are you doing, fool?" he said, snatching the book from my hands.

I could feel tears welling up in my eyes. When I shook my head, they began to leak down my cheeks.

"We're worried about you, Sadiq, man. We're scared, Fatima and me, about what you're getting into."

"It's nothing that concerns you. And you

can tell our sister to stop interfering as well."

He was holding the still-open scrapbook by his side and I could see George Smith's face staring up at me.

"Why have you got all that stuff in there? All those newspaper articles and things?"

"Because, Omar, you have to know your enemy, and George Smith is our enemy. He wants war with the Muslims. He wants to drive us out of this precious country of his."

I shook my head. We'd been talking about the elections at school.

"He won't be allowed to do that, Sadiq. There are lots of other more sensible politicians who will stop him if he tries anything."

Sadiq snorted.

"I don't have any faith in politicians. Sometimes you have to act for yourself."

I could feel myself getting angry now. The skin at the sides of my head seemed to be all stretched and prickly.

"So what do you and your friends plan to do, Sadiq? Blow him up or something?"

I suppose I expected my big brother to laugh at what I'd said, but instead he just looked away from me and stared out the window. Droplets of rain were dribbling down it in erratic little streams.

"Come on, Sadiq. Answer me."

Sadiq rolled his shoulders and then his neck.

"Please answer me."

Finally he let out a long sigh.

"Omar, let's just pretend we never had this conversation. And don't you mention it to Fatima, either."

GEORGIE

When I got back from the hospital – where it took them six hours to decide there was nothing obvious wrong with me – the house was quiet. Albion, my sister, was over at her friend's place and I guessed that Dad must be slumped in his den watching The History Channel with a cigar and a couple of bottles of real ale. Mum fussed about in the kitchen, desperate to fix me something to eat. She must have been starving because she'd eaten nothing all afternoon while we waited for the doctors to do the scans and blood tests and half-hearted quizzing about whether I was worried or depressed or something. I sensed she was getting angry that Dad hadn't come out to check on me, though she had sent him a text from the hospital to say I was basically OK. Finally he appeared in the doorway of his den with a documentary about the Battle of Stalingrad rumbling and flickering on the television screen behind him.

"So what do they reckon?" he asked, hitching up his jogging bottoms.

"They don't know, George. We've been there all afternoon and they haven't got a clue what's going on with him."

"Did any of the doctors give you grief, like when Albion broke her arm?"

"No, they were fine. They didn't make the connection with you."

He rolled his bottom lip.

"Did you have to wait long?"

Mum got some lettuce from the fridge and began to wash it under the tap.

"I said, did you have to wait long?"

Mum turned the tap off and glared at him. The muscle that twitches in her jaw when she's tense was fluttering like a trapped moth.

"You mean was the hospital full of doctors from India and Africa who couldn't speak English? And were the waiting rooms clogged up with asylum-seekers? No. Not that I noticed, George."

"It was a straightforward question."

My mum blew a strand of blond hair away from her face.

"I thought you was trying to make a political point as usual."

Dad rubbed the dark whiskers on his chin. He really needed to shave twice a day.

"I think you'll find it's 'you *were* trying to make a political point', not 'you was'," he growled.

Mum threw the dripping lettuce into the sink and stormed out of the kitchen.

"Whatever," she called over her shoulder.

Dad looked at me and shrugged, as if to say, "What was that all about?" But their arguments had been growing much more frequent lately. Mum didn't really care about politics, but you couldn't be in George Smith's family and stay on the sidelines. You got dragged right into the boggy parts of the pitch every day of your life.

Dad pulled up a stool next to mine at the breakfast bar. Neither of us said anything. The noise of a loan company's TV advert filtered through from the den.

"So what happened? I spoke to Mr Atkinson who says you had a run-in with some Jewish kid and then you fainted when he sent you to apologise. Is that right?"

I nodded.

"Pretty much."

"So that's the second time now you've had a bit of a wobble, like at the rally in Barking. I don't understand."

"Perhaps I'm not as tough as you and Brian and Tony and Mart."

"Forget them. By the sounds of it, you're about as tough as Billy Elliot."

He grinned, and there was that sparkle in his eye which often charmed even the news journalists who expected to despise him for his political views.

"Come here."

He reached around the back of my neck and pulled me close to him. Dad was smaller than average but he was a solid block of muscle. He kissed the top of my head and I smelt the fumes from the beer he'd been drinking.

"Who loves ya?" he said.

"You do," I whispered.

"Louder."

"You do."

"That's right. Now I'm going to have a sarnie, whatever anyone else plans to eat this evening. D'you want one?"

"I'm OK."

Dad enjoyed doing stuff in the kitchen. He always made sure he had everything he needed all laid out precisely, even if he was just making something simple like a cheese and onion sandwich. With a look of great concentration on his face, he pressed the onion down on the chopping board as if he was daring it to try and slip free from his grasp. When he'd chopped it into little bits, he reached for a different knife to set about the cheddar.

"Sir Oswald Mosley," I said. "Tell me some more about him."

"You're asking the right man. I reckon I know everything there is to know about Mosley."

He smiled, then his brow became creased.

"Has that Mr Stokes been having a go again?"

"Something like that."

"Well, despite what Mr Stokes would have you believe, Mosley was a great Englishman. He was the leader of the British Union of Fascists, the Blackshirts. And a lot of people saw the sense in what he was saying about the problems in our country in the 1930s. You know that paper your mother reads, the *Daily Mail*? They ran a headline which said 'Hurrah for the Blackshirts', so even people in the mainstream supported Mosley and his ideas. Mosley wanted to march with his supporters down Cable Street in the East End of London to protest about the way the country was being taken over by the Jews, just like it's being overrun by the Muslims now. And, as I think I've told you before, there was a big ruck and a lot of property got smashed up because a crowd of Jews and their Communist friends blocked the road and stopped them going through."

"Mr Stokes reckons there were a lot of ordinary local people who decided to stand with the Jews. Thousands were there, he said, forming a human barricade."

"Maybe so. A lot of misguided locals who should have known better."

"And Mosley was stopped and turned back?"

Dad shrugged.

"Yeah, he was stopped. But if the police had done their job properly, the Blackshirts would've been allowed to march right through and make their lawful protest."

I heard a noise, and looked up to see Albion slinking in through the back door. Her friend

Lulu's place was only three houses away and she spent most of her time there.

"All right?" she said to me.

"All right."

"I hear you had another funny turn or something."

"I'm fine now. Pretty much back to normal."

"Normal, Georgie boy? There's no such thing as normal in this house."

Albion pulled a face at Dad, which made her look like a sulky Barbie doll, then she flounced through the kitchen and headed up the stairs to her room. I waited for the clatter of her heels to fade away, then I glanced up at Dad. Should I say it or not? He was my father, after all.

"Erm, I'm pretty sure I heard that girl's voice in my head again. That Fatima."

Dad put his half-eaten sandwich down on the plate. Then he jabbed at me with a stubby index finger.

"Don't start up with that nonsense, Georgie.

You made a fool of yourself in Barking. The boys couldn't get over all that Fatima stuff. It was bad enough you talking about hearing voices without them getting the idea it was some Muslim girlie you were daydreaming about. I don't want that name mentioned in this house again. Not ever."

He pushed his stool back and stomped off to his den, slamming the door shut behind him.

"Fatima," I whispered, after he'd gone.

FATIMA

People often ask me if I can see something. Anything. Like little points of light that dance about or blurry shapes that move as slowly as fish in a darkened aquarium. They find it hard to imagine seeing nothing at all. "Is it like at night when there are no stars and everything's black?" Omar asked me once, when he was six or seven. I said, "Yes, sweetest, it's just like that."

But I wasn't really being truthful. I've never seen colours: black and white and everything in between mean nothing to me. Take an orange, my favourite fruit. I can tell you what it feels like when I sink my teeth into the juicy flesh and the sweetness dribbles down my chin. But orange – the colour? I'm never going to get that.

I don't often feel sorry for myself. When you're blind, it's hard to do all sorts of things but your other senses become stronger somehow and much more sensitive. I can tell just by the sound of Sadiq's footsteps on the hall floor if he's in a good mood or not. When our mother laughs, I can hear if she's really covering up another disappointment about her life here in England. When the men from Tower Hamlets come to collect the rubbish, I know them all from their voices. If one of them is whistling, I can say who it is – it's usually Jermaine! Late at night when my father comes home from the restaurant, I can untangle all the different aromas from his hair and skin and clothes, and tell him the last meal he prepared – usually it's mutton vindaloo for one of the City workers.

When you're blind, you have to reach out to the world – you can't just take it in through your eyes. From the time I was very young

I was aware of other minds existing beyond the edges of my own – like distant planets in other universes. I could sense all the millions of brains across London pulsing and bleeping away like a vast computer network. Except that they weren't linked up together. As a little girl I sent out my thoughts like wispy spiders' webs floating on a breeze. Then other people's thoughts started coming back to me, and I never felt lonely again.

Most people can't hear me and I can't connect with them. There's a girl I speak to called Melissa, who says I'm like Fatima FM Radio, but not everyone can tune into it! I don't want to joke about my gift. I know it's special and important. I want to heal people with it, though I forget sometimes that it has the power to hurt, too. When I'm desperate to talk to someone, or they're trying to block me out, I do the equivalent of screaming at the top of my lungs. Then they feel intense pain. Sometimes they just shut themselves down. That's when I try to soothe them.

My name is Fatima. I know that you can hear me. Please don't be afraid.

I want to do good with my gift. Along with all the evil in the world there really is a lot of good too, and some of it is where you don't expect to find it. As my teacher's favourite poet, John Masefield, said, "I have seen flowers come in stony places. And kind things done by men with ugly faces." Of course, the way I look at it there is no ugly or beautiful, no fat or thin, no black or white or brown. I may be blind to what you can see, but I know what goes on in people's heads and hearts. And, of course, that's what really matters.

My name is Fatima. I know that you can hear me. Please don't be afraid.

GEORGIE

Lunchtime at Caddogan Hall and the dining area was packed, steamy and noisy. I scanned the room with its oil paintings, traditional wood panelling and modern, cheap-looking, tables and chairs. There was nowhere to sit apart from with a group of girls in my year, so, without asking or making eye contact or anything, I put my tray down and started eating a portion of plain pasta. It was all I could face.

You know how it is, you can't help earwigging other people's conversations and though I had no real interest in Emily, Lydia and some new, dark-haired girl who was sitting with them, their chit-chat kept interrupting my daydreaming. The new girl was called Inge – if I'd heard it right – and she was from South Africa. But it seemed she wasn't just an ordinary South African, she was what she called "a South African with a conscience". Great, I thought, I'm going to spend my lunchtime listening to some rich white girl whining about how unfair it is that she's been born with so many privileges while the poor blacks are living in poverty.

Of course, blond-airhead Emily, whose father was from South Africa too, just wanted to talk about the *awesome* safaris she'd been on, the miles of *stunning* golden beaches and the *fantastic* restaurants along the sea front in Durban. If it wasn't for all the crime in her father's homeland, she and her family would go back there *like a shot*.

I sensed that Inge was getting uncomfortable.

"Yah, Emily, but the thing is, for years we whites treated everyone else like second-class citizens. They couldn't swim from the same part of the beach as us. They couldn't eat in the same restaurants…"

Lydia looked across and caught me staring at the three of them. A smile animated her pouty little mouth.

"Of course, if Georgie's dad had his way, this country would be run on the same lines."

Inge looked puzzled, a slight frown creasing her high white forehead. I decided it might be best if I made the introductions myself.

"I'm Georgie. My dad George Smith is a right-wing politician whose money is good enough for Caddogan Hall but whose political views everyone seems to hate."

"He's not just a right-winger," Lydia said acidly, "he's the leader of the Fascist Party."

She flicked back the curtain of red hair that usually hung across her eyes and stared at me triumphantly.

"OK," Inge said, slowly drawing out those two letters as though she needed some time to think about this unexpected information.

"My parents are actually very right wing too. They say things about black people that make my skin crawl. But what about you, Georgie, what do you stand for?"

Lydia was desperate to butt in again.

"You should ask Adam Rosen. He might give you an interesting insight into Georgie and what makes him tick."

I put my fork down on the tray. The pasta tasted suddenly as if it was made from wallpaper paste. When I finally spoke, I found I was saying stuff I'd never said before.

"The thing is, Inge, you can't choose your parents, can you? I didn't ask to have George Smith as a dad. I suppose what's important is to know your own mind, to be your own person."

Lydia snorted, her nostrils flaring like a horse's.

"I can't believe I'm hearing this. Everyone knows you're exactly the same as your dad. You don't hang around with anyone at Caddogan Hall who isn't white. And you've never had any friends who are black or Asian or whatever."

I wanted to pick up the tray and hurl it at Lydia, but suddenly I felt a cool, tingly sensation in my head as though my brain was being washed in bubbly spring water. Then I heard the girl's voice, only this time it wasn't like a thousand, deafening decibels. It was quiet, barely audible, and soothing.

I'd be happy to be your friend.

Despite everything I'd grown up with, the thought suddenly struck me as a perfectly reasonable idea. So I announced it to the three of them, just as if I was thinking out loud.

"I have a friend called Fatima."

Emily and Lydia looked doubtful. Inge had this expression on her milk white face that said, "Good for you, Georgie".

"I don't believe him for a second," Lydia said smugly.

"Isn't that like a Muslim name?" Emily asked.

I stood up.

"I don't care what you think. I am my own person, and I do have a friend who happens to be called Fatima."

When I reached the hatch where we scraped off the leftovers and dumped our trays, who should be in front of me but Adam Rosen himself? Could this day get any worse? I was pretty sure he'd seen me out of the corner of his still-swollen eye, but he didn't acknowledge that I was there.

I coughed.

"Er, Rosen. I mean Adam. Do you have a moment?"

He turned towards me, but I couldn't read the look on his face. Was he frightened, hostile?

"I never actually shook your hand and apologised – what with me collapsing and everything. I wanted to say sorry for hitting you. And I also wanted to say, don't judge me on what you know about my father. He's my dad, so I'm not going to publicly denounce him or whatever it was you said

I should do. But I don't think the same way he does. Not any more. And I'm not sure I ever really did."

Adam Rosen took my hand and shook it. Then he seemed to remember something and reached into the pocket of his blazer. He pulled out a crumpled booklet and held it out to me. On the front it said *The Battle of Cable Street 1936.* There was a grainy black and white picture of policemen and local East Enders and a barricade that had been built across the road to stop Mosley and his Blackshirts from marching through.

"I'll forgive you, Smith," he said, "But I want you to read this. Don't just throw it away, read it. Then you'll see why I have a problem with your father."

MELISSA

Everything changed for me the day Fatima told me she was blind. We were basically having this row, because she reckoned I had to make more of an effort with people. She said I was rude, which was true, and spoilt, which wasn't really the case because my mum never gave me anything much apart from sweets. I told Fatima I was sick of having someone so perfect try and tell me what to do.

But I'm not perfect, Melissa. And one day I might need you to support and guide me.

I didn't believe her. How could I possibly be of any use to her?

*I might need you to be my eyes, Melissa.
I might need to lean on you.*

I suddenly got all panicky and asked her
if she was sick or something, but she said she
wasn't ill: she just happened to be blind. I was
shocked at first. But then I started to see that
maybe I really could help her. Worthless as
I was, I might actually be useful to Fatima.
That was a good feeling, I swear.

I told her I would change, that I would
be a better person. She insisted I had to start
with my learning support assistant, Stacey.
That wasn't exactly what I wanted to hear
because Stacey had broken up with Reece
and was all miserable and snuffly when she
was working with me in school. Stacey was a
real downer, but to be honest, I hadn't helped.
I'd told her I'd seen Reece walking past the
Railway Tavern with his arm round another
girl, and she'd run out of the classroom in tears.
When I said I'd made it up just for a laugh, she
wouldn't see the funny side, and told Miss de
Souza she needed a break from me for a bit.

The thing about Fatima is, she sees the good in everyone. She reckons that even people you think of as bad are capable of doing wonderful things. Like some bloke who goes to the football or nightclubs and gets in fights all the time might be the one who risks his life to rescue you when your house is on fire. I can't say that's true from my experience, but that's what Fatima thinks.

Making an effort with Stacey was easier than I thought it would be. I did have to bite my tongue not to say spiteful things, but mostly I managed to be nice.

"You're bound to get back with Reece or find someone even better," I told her. "Someone as skinny and pretty as you could have anyone they want."

She gave me this brave smile and said, "So you was definitely making it up about him and that girl Vicky?"

"I was just having a laugh. You're so easy to wind up, Stace."

Thanks to Fatima, now there was no

stopping me. I started sitting on the buddy bench at break-times and if people came and sat with me to be kind, I'd try hard to be kind back.

One time I called out to Kele as he was going by.

"Oi Kel, over here!"

"What do you want?"

"I just want to say sorry for being a pain all the time."

He stopped bouncing his basketball and held it against his hip.

"What's the punchline?"

"It's not a joke. I'm trying to change. I really want to be a better person. Innit everyone's got a right to change?"

Kele chuckled to himself.

"OK, Melissa, I accept your apology. You are weird, though."

I smiled my dazzling, one-hundred-watt smile.

"Thank you, Kel, I love you too."

Kele flipped the basketball up in the air and

started bouncing it again.

"See you then, Kel."

"Yeah, Melissa, I'll see you around."

He walked off towards the netball hoop, laughing and shaking his head.

See, Fatima, I thought to myself, *I hear you and I do take notice of what you say*.

OMAR

Everything about that night was different. I remember waking and seeing the red digits on my alarm clock glowing like neon in the darkness: 2:00. That confused me. I was pretty sure I'd never been anything other than deep asleep at two in the morning before. Then I became aware of my big brother whimpering. I'd never known him to cry and he sounded pitiful, like a frightened animal, a young stag, maybe, that had escaped from wolves but might yet die from its wounds. I'm not sure I really thought of predators and prey at the time. It might have been something that came later when Sadiq told me about the beating he'd taken and his fear of what might happen next.

I reached for the bedside lamp and clicked it on. His bed was in shadow against the far wall of the room and his body was turned away from me. He seemed to be lying fully-clothed on top of the covers with his legs pulled up to his chest.

"Turn it off, man," he groaned. "It's hurting my eyes."

I got out of my bed and moved hesitantly across the carpet to him. His left shoulder was shaking and I touched it lightly with my fingers.

"Sadiq, what's wrong? Please tell me what's the matter with you."

He was silent for a few moments, then he whispered, "I'm a dead man, little brother. I probably shouldn't have come home because I could put you all in danger, but I didn't know where else to go."

He rolled over awkwardly to squint up at me, and I remember gasping. He was barely

recognisable. In the yellow light cast by the lamp, the blood on his face and clothes was dark, almost black. His nose had been flattened and seemed like it belonged to someone else. I just stared at him with my mouth open.

"You think maybe I've lost my film star good looks?" he said finally.

Sadiq hadn't joked in months – all his talk had been of politics and religion. I tried to smile.

"You were never that good-looking anyway, man."

He actually laughed then, but it started him coughing so much, it sounded as though he was going to bring up one of his lungs or something.

"Who did this to you?"

For a second I thought he wasn't going to say, but then he sighed deeply as though it didn't matter any more whether he told me or not.

"That guy George Smith, the Fascist, the one in the newspaper cuttings. . ."

"His people did this to you?"

He shook his head, although it clearly pained him even to move.

"Hush, Omar. I'll explain, but don't interrupt me."

I nodded, and sat down on the corner of his bed.

"These men I've been hanging out with, they're extreme, I think you know that. They're planning to kill him. They know where he lives. They know his habits, where he goes each day. They've got this device with a timer, like an alarm clock, that's going to go off and blow up his car. *Kaboom*. No more George Smith."

"Which would be a good thing. . ."

"Which in many ways would be a good thing. He hates Muslims, all of us, even children like Fatima and you. But it's murder, Omar. I thought I could go along with it but now that it's actually happening, I don't have the stomach for it."

"They can't make you do anything, Sadiq."

He shifted his legs, trying to get more comfortable.

"No, they can't make me. But, as you can see, they're not happy about me pulling out. I was only supposed to drive them up to Smith's place in Hertfordshire. I said I couldn't do it, and to them that's a betrayal they can't forgive. I thought they were going to kill me. And they may well yet, but their minds are focused on what's going to happen tomorrow morning."

I was desperately trying to come up with a solution, a plan or something.

"What about the police, Sadiq? Why don't you go to them now and say what these men are going to do?"

"Because they'll put me in prison for ever. They'll think I'm just as bad as the others. They won't thank me, pat me on the back and send me home. They'll know I've been mixing with terrorists. They'll call me a terrorist too, which I suppose is what I am."

"You're not a terrorist, Sadiq. You may have

got mixed up in something stupid, you may not have been thinking straight, but you're a good person. You're my big brother, the one I used to play cricket with, the one who taught me how to spin a ball so that hardly anyone can hit it."

Sadiq started crying softly again.

"I don't know who or what I am any more, Omar. I just know I'm scared and I don't know what to do."

And then it came to me, like fireworks suddenly lighting up the night sky.

"Fatima," I said. "Fatima can help."

Sadiq stopped crying and tried, with great care, to blow his swollen nose.

"Please don't tell Fatima. I don't want her to be worried. I know she's special but, unless she can speak directly to George Smith, I'm afraid he's a dead man. Just like me."

GEORGIE

In the rainforest steam of our kitchen, I leafed through the booklet that Adam Rosen had given me at school. He'd got inside my head all right, and so had the grainy black and white pictures of the Battle of Cable Street. I kept looking at one of Sir Oswald Mosley strutting about with his fascist followers. Mosley was tall and posh-looking, nothing like my father, but I could imagine Dad in that same black uniform with the peaked cap and shiny boots, goose-stepping around the country like he owned it. Other pictures showed Jewish shops all boarded up, ready for the violence that the Fascists would bring. I saw the cramped, tumble-down houses where the Jewish people lived alongside other East Enders, many of whom had come originally from Ireland. Cable Street and its poor, besieged immigrants seemed a million miles from my own mansion-like home.

I was startled by a sudden noise and looked up to find that Dad had emerged, blinking like a small sleepy bear, from the dark of his den. He shuffled across the kitchen floor in his dressing-gown and slippers. Mum claimed he was suffering from what she called "man flu", though his sea-lion's cough sounded real enough to me, and worse than you'd get with a normal cold. He lifted the lids of the three saucepans that were hissing and bubbling on top of Mum's new self-cleaning oven and grunted unhappily. Then he began rooting around in the depths of the fridge. At last he emerged with a more cheerful look on his face and a large slab of chocolate in his fist.

"Don't tell your mother," he wheezed.

We sat in near-silence, broken only by the soothing burble from the stove and the spluttering sounds Dad made when he ate. Then he gestured for me to pass him Adam Rosen's booklet. At first he seemed pleased – he liked me to take an interest in politics and history, and was always trying to get me to watch his documentaries with him. But as he scanned the pages, two frown lines, like deep, dark trenches, creased his brow.

"Where d'you get this garbage, Georgie?"

"It's about Mosley."

"I said, where did you get it? Was it Mr Stokes? This is all from the Jews' point of view. It's Jewish propaganda. What Mr Stokes won't tell you is that the Jews were taking over our country and stealing what was rightfully ours. No one wanted them here. Jobs and houses that should have gone to English people were going to them instead. What you've got to understand about the Jews is that they're arrogant, they think they're special, and they'll try and take over the whole world if people like us don't stop them."

I grabbed the booklet back from him. The pages were damp from the steam of the cooking. Surely it wasn't all made up. It seemed believable to me and, in this version of history, the Blackshirts were the bad guys, the Jews their innocent victims.

"But Dad, no one else would have wanted to live in these houses. They're slums. It says here the Jews came to this country to work hard and make a better life for themselves. What's so bad about that? They were prepared to start from nothing."

"No . . . one . . . wanted . . . them . . . here," he spat out the words slowly. Each one seemed to be coated in venom. I couldn't think when he'd ever used such a hostile tone with me.

"When it comes down to it, Georgie, it's all about race – everything is. It's about keeping our white race strong and pure. The Jews and the Muslims want to destroy us. And we've got to take action to stop them."

I felt sweaty and light-headed, as if I too

had the flu, but I was determined to make my point to him.

"You say no one wanted them here, but how come so many ordinary English people were prepared to stand up for them? It was thousands of ordinary English people who helped block off Cable Street so the Fascists couldn't march down it and frighten and intimidate the Jews who lived there. Look at these banners they're carrying: 'They shall not pass'. That's your precious Blackshirts they're talking about."

"No . . . one . . . wanted . . . them . . . here."

This time his voice was much louder and he leant towards me and pushed his index finger into my chest. It hurt, but although I was frightened, I heard myself laugh a weird, twisted sort of laugh.

"Don't push me. That's what fascists like you do, isn't it Dad? If you can't win an argument, you start threatening people."

He stared at me with those famous blue eyes. When he finally spoke, he sounded calm and in control.

"Not fascists like me, Georgie. Fascists like us. You need to remember whose side you're on."

I thought that was it, but he hadn't finished. I sensed a blur of movement out of the corner of my left eye, then felt a searing pain across my cheek. For a second I thought he'd taken a serving spoon from one of the simmering pans and held it against my face. Anything seemed possible suddenly. But it was a slap from his right hand that had stung me. He flexed his fingers and examined his palm as though it was something unfamiliar to him.

"You made me do that," he said. "Now go to your room."

That night my dreams were filled with images of my dad and his followers dressed in the Blackshirt uniform. But though their faces were still recognisable to me, Brian, Mart, Tony and all the rest looked like huge lizards. They had scaly skin and long slithery tongues that kept sliding out of their reptile snouts. They walked unsteadily on their back legs through a ramshackle street market that I didn't recognise. The market traders and shopkeepers were terrified, of course, and either ran into the backs of their shops or hid behind their stalls. I watched transfixed as my lizard-like dad scooped up half a chicken from behind a counter and began to tear it apart with his fangs; a mixture of juice and drool hung in a long string from his jaws. Then he swished his crocodile tail and knocked over a crate of oranges which bounced and rolled like giant marbles into the gutter.

A little Asian girl in a red plastic raincoat began to scream, her brown eyes wide with terror. At first I thought she was just howling but then I realised she was actually forming words: *Go away, monster. Go away, monster.* I bent down so that I was closer to her level, all the time making soothing noises. I was trying to tell her not to be afraid, that I would protect her from these evil creatures. But then I looked at my own hands and shuddered to see that they too were covered in reptilian scales; my fingers had become claws.

"No!" I began to shout, and the effort woke me. I lay on my bed in a tangle of blankets, sweating and breathless.

I stared at the ceiling for what felt like hours, fearful of what further tricks my mind might play if I was to fall back to sleep. Close to dawn, I dropped into a heavy, dreamless stupor. When I woke, I fumbled for the alarm clock, then let out a long moan. I'd never been this late for school before.

From the kitchen came the sound of an argument that was already in full swing.

"Look, if you're too ill to drive him, I'll go."

Mum was unloading the dishwasher, crashing around like she was giving the pots and pans a good work-out.

"He's got to have some breakfast first, though. He didn't eat a thing last night with you sending him to bed and all. He must be starving and upset as well, with you shouting at him."

And hitting him, I thought. It seemed Mum was unaware of exactly what had passed between Dad and me.

"Leave it out, Doreen, will you? I'm up now, aren't I? I'll drive him to school. After he's had some breakfast."

They both became aware of me standing barefoot in the doorway.

"Morning, darling," Mum said. "You're making me feel cold without your slippers. What can I get you to eat?"

Dad gave me a goofy, lopsided grin and came towards me boxer-like, pretend-jabbing with his left arm as he moved. When he reached me, he pulled me to his chest and I smelled shower-gel and aftershave and that scent I'd recognise anywhere that made him my dad.

"Who loves ya?" he said.

What could I say?

"You do."

"Have you got over our little disagreement last night? I've been thinking about it and I'm proud my boy's starting to form his own opinions. They're all wrong, of course…"

He winked, then coughed.

"You just need to spend more time with your old man so you can see why it is that I'm right. Why the British Fascists are right. And why we'll win in the end."

He escorted me, arm around my shoulder, to my usual seat at the breakfast bar and picked up a mug of Lemsip he'd been drinking. He swallowed the dregs of it and winced.

"Have your breakfast, Georgie, then come out and find me. I'll be in the car listening to the radio, trying to keep up with world events."

He gave a mirthless smile to my mum. She always had the kitchen radio tuned to a soppy music station in the mornings.

I didn't really have time to eat anything but Mum insisted. I spooned some cornflakes that tasted like bits of sodden cardboard into my mouth and gulped down a mug of watery tea.

As I was getting dressed, I realised that I would normally be halfway on the journey to school by now. I thought of sending Albion a text. She'd started travelling to school with her friend Lulu every day – anything to avoid my dad. Maybe she could pass on a message to my tutor. There was no point asking Mark or Scooter, they'd almost certainly be late themselves.

I let Mum kiss me on the cheek and straighten my tie, then I left the suffocating warmth of the house and started walking down the drive.

A flock of birds, crows or rooks or something were wheeling and complaining above a copse of trees in the farmer's field opposite. I saw the silhouette of Dad's head and shoulders through the Range Rover's tinted glass windows. He was sitting where he loved to be, high up in the driver's seat. His car towered over most other vehicles on the road and Mum often said he would have been much happier living in it. When he first bought it, she'd joked about what she'd called "small man syndrome": because Dad was shorter than average, she reckoned he liked being above the rest of the traffic to make up for it. That hadn't gone down well and she'd never mentioned it again.

I realised as I neared the Range Rover that I'd left my pencil-case amid the clutter on the desk in my bedroom. I was about to turn back for it, but a glance at my watch told me there was no time. I reached out for the passenger side door handle, and that's when I heard a voice. I spun round, squinting back at the house to see if it was Mum calling me. But she was indoors in the living room behind the double-glazed picture window.

You are in great danger. Please don't get into the car.

The voice was clear and insistent, and took me totally by surprise. It swirled like a cool current around my brain, and I shook my head, as though I was trying to remove bath water from my ears.

This is Fatima. I know that you can hear me. You and your father must get away from the car. Please, it's very important.

My first thought was one of relief that the

voice was not hurting me. Twice now it had been bearable and had not caused any pain. Then I considered the meaning of the words I was hearing. Was I really in danger? It seemed ridiculous. Surely this Fatima was just the work of an overactive imagination. My dreams of the night before had shown me how feverish my mind could be.

I took hold of the handle and squeezed it. The door opened softly and I heard a politician's voice on the radio, smarmy and wheedling. The interviewer was aggressive and kept trying to interrupt him.

"Hurry up, Georgie boy. It'll be time to fetch you home soon."

I opened my mouth to speak and then a huge wrecking ball of noise smacked me between the eyes.

I TOLD YOU NOT TO GET IN THE CAR! YOU MUST GET AWAY FROM IT, BOTH OF YOU!

I staggered backwards and found myself sitting down on the gravel with my rucksack in my lap.

Dad leaned across the cream-coloured passenger seat to get a better view of me. He looked tiny suddenly, like a jockey sitting on top of one of those enormous shire horses.

"What is it now, Georgie?"

Fatima had got my attention. I felt winded and sick. If I didn't do what I was told, there was every chance that she would attack me again. My words came out all shrill and whiny, like a six year old begging for sweets.

"Dad, this is going to sound mental, but we need to get away from the car."

He banged down with the heel of his hand on the steering wheel, making the whole car shudder. His face had started to turn tomato-red.

"You're right, it sounds utterly bonkers. Get your backside in here!"

"Please Dad, you've got to get out of there. I'm hearing that voice again, that Fatima, and she says we're in danger."

The wrecking ball returned for another

swing at me:

THERE IS A BOMB ATTACHED UNDERNEATH THE CAR. YOU MUST RUN NOW!

I staggered to my feet and sprinted round the bonnet of the Range Rover. When I reached the driver's door I yanked it open and began clawing at my dad's clothing. He lost his balance and slid halfway out, but his seat belt wouldn't let him fall the whole way. I grabbed his right ear, which felt hot and rubbery in my hand, and started pulling on it until I felt it might rip away from the side of his head.

"Get out of there, Dad. Just do it, please!"

Suddenly he was freed from the seat belt and sprawled on the gravel beside me, but I still had his ear and some of his hair in my grip. He was cursing and flapping at me with one arm, trying to push me away.

"Now run!" I shouted, and we did, him half-crouching as I dragged him, off-balance, in the direction of the house.

I glanced up and saw my mum at the

living-room window, staring out at us with a look of utter confusion on her face. She was chewing on a strand of her blond hair as though she might bite right through it.

It was then that all the sounds in the world came together in one great roar that rolled over me like a huge tidal wave. For a moment I wondered if it could be Fatima's voice shouting again, but then I saw hunks of metal from the car flying past us, some embedding themselves in the wall of the house, where they smoked like fallen asteroids.

A great orange fire-ball reflected in the window where Mum was still standing. For some reason, that would make no sense at all to the anti-terrorism police, the picture window didn't shatter and I was able to watch as my dad and I flew in seeming slow-motion onto the stretch of lawn to the side of the drive. I'd let go of his ear by this point, but we still landed together in a jumble of limbs. The explosion didn't leave either of us deaf, even temporarily, but at first I thought the

world had gone silent.

Then the birds in the trees over the way resumed their mad squawking. I heard my dad's voice all husky with cold, or maybe with fear.

"How did you know that was going to happen?"

He was staring, unblinking, at the twisted wreckage of his car and the angry black cloud that billowed above it. I had the strangest urge to start giggling – the doctors explained later that's because I was in shock.

"Seriously, Dad, you've got to listen to me more," I said, with tears of laughter in my eyes.

He was groaning now because he'd cracked a few ribs. Apart from some scratches, I was completely unharmed. Suddenly Mum was there and it seemed she'd been struck dumb. She hugged us both but couldn't say a thing. Instead I heard Fatima's voice speaking faintly inside me, like a butterfly batting its wings against the folds of my brain.

I am so glad you're safe. All I ever wanted for this world is peace.

But Fatima did not have the last word. My dad, grimacing with pain, managed to raise himself up on one elbow.

"I promise you, this is the work of the Muslims," he whispered hoarsely to no one in particular. "They talk about holy wars and jihads, but they will not have seen the like of what I've got planned for them. As God is my witness, I am going into battle. I will get my revenge."

MELISSA

Well, Stacey, my learning support assistant, and her ex-boyfriend Reece got back together. Then they decided to get married. But that wasn't the amazing bit. What was really amazing was that Stacey asked me to be her bridesmaid.

"How many bridesmaids are you having, then?" I said.

"Just the one," she answered, her eyes all shiny, "and it's you!"

I asked my teacher Miss de Souza if it was a reward because my behaviour had improved "out of all recognition". But Miss de Souza laughed and said this wasn't about house-points or Star of the Week badges.

"It's because she really likes you as a person. That's not always been the case, Melissa. It shows how far you've come."

Of course, Leona had to be spiteful in front of the whole class.

"Everyone, yeah, imagine Stacey's wedding photos. There'll be Stacey and Reece looking like a couple of midgets and this giant bridesmaid next to them."

"Innit, though!" chorused Kodi and Simone.

Miss de Souza was about to jump in with, "Oi, no put-downs!" and tell them they were totally out of order, but I just smiled the sweetest smile.

"Girls," I said, "I feel sorry for you that you're not able to share in my happiness. Actually, I think I'll look stunning in a bridesmaid's outfit!"

Miss de Souza and the rest of the class burst out laughing, but not at me – it was *with* me this time. I could tell they were on my side. Leona, Kodi and Simone just opened and closed their mouths like three goldfish because they couldn't think of anything to say back.

It wasn't a line I'd got from Fatima, but it was the kind of thing I could imagine her saying – all calm and confident. I suppose it also showed how much my social skills had improved, because in the past I'd have pushed over their table, grabbed one of Leona's stupid girly pigtails and tried to rip it off her head.

GEORGIE

After the car bomb attack I heard other voices, children's voices, whispering to me day and night. They were not as strong and clear as Fatima's and sometimes they were hard to understand. But they were insistent, like fluttering sounds made by the wings of small birds.

Can you hear me? My name is Chesley. I'm glad you're all right, man.

This is Aamina. Fatima told me what happened. It sounded terrible. I mean, you could have been killed.

I'm John. You don't know me, but I'm thinking about you . . . you know, wishing you well.

There are lots of us, Georgie. We want to help you.

And then I'd hear Fatima herself.

You must stay strong, Georgie. You must believe in yourself. Sometimes flowers grow in stony places. Never forget that.

To my family, I seemed lost in daydreams. Albion soon got bored of me. Mum stared blankly and said it would take a long while for us all to "heal emotionally". She spent most of the day watching TV and popping pills the doctor had given her. They kept her as placid as a tranquilized sheep.

And Dad? Dad was angry. The more zombie-like Mum became, the more animated he got. He just wouldn't rest. His anger blazed behind his eyes and spewed from his mouth in curses and complaints. And he stoked that anger. He poured fuel on it. He fanned the flames until it seemed they would flare up and consume us all. Part of me was angry too, but I couldn't help thinking that Dad had brought this upon us.

We'd heard from the anti-terrorism police that a group of Islamic extremists had claimed responsibility for the car bomb attack. In a statement on a website, they'd warned they would try again.

Dad didn't seem concerned.

"Bring it on. Let's see them flush themselves out. I'd love the chance to get at them. I'd just love it."

All the time he was formulating plans. He'd be on the phone to Brian and others whose voices I recognised. But he also spent hours talking to shadowy figures I'd never heard of, men who were cagey about giving their names when I happened to take their calls.

Dad wanted to hit back at the terrorists, frighten them like they'd frightened us, see them dead if he could. But even that wouldn't bring an end to his anger. Dad also wanted to make a statement to every Muslim in the country.

Finally he announced what he planned to do and it made me shudder. That's because I knew it was all my fault. If it hadn't been for me and Adam Rosen's booklet, I doubt he'd ever have thought of it.

"October the Fourth, Georgie — what's important about that date?"

I was toying with some scrambled eggs Mum had made for me, pushing the pale yellow gloop around my plate with a fork.

"Is it Grandad's birthday?"

"That's on the twelfth."

"Something to do with World War Two — the Battle of Stalingrad or something."

"You're getting warmer. It is to do with a battle, but much closer to home. The Battle of Cable Street."

I could sense the excitement in his voice, but I didn't guess where he was going with this.

"On October the Fourth, 1936, Sir Oswald Mosley and the British Union of Fascists tried to march down Cable Street, but they were stopped. On October the Fourth this year I'm going to finish the job — do it properly."

I put the fork down and glanced up at him. He looked re-energised. He'd combed his hair and had a shave, after days of shambling around the house like a tramp in a dressing-gown.

"Why would you want to do that? I thought the Jews had gone from that part of London."

"Indeed they have, Georgie boy, but the Muslims have moved in. Cable Street is crawling with them. And it's time they tasted a bit of fear – time they looked out their windows and saw hundreds of Fascists marching by, reclaiming the streets for the white man."

"No one's going to let you do that. Don't you need permission to have a march?"

He let out a rasping laugh.

"No one's going to tell me where I can and can't go in my own country. We won't ask anybody's permission. We'll just turn up. It'll be a surprise for them. We'll show them they're not wanted here, just like Mosley tried to show the Jews. And another thing – I want my family with me. I want those Muslims to see a proud white family at the front of the march."

It was my turn to laugh.

"There's no way Mum and Albion will go

with you. Anyway, it's probably going to get violent. Do you really want them there if it all kicks off?"

He rubbed his newly-smooth chin with his fingers.

"Maybe not. I'll think about it. But what about you, Georgie? Will you come? I wouldn't ask if it wasn't important to me. You're my son, after all. My son and heir."

His blue eyes were sparkling, not dead as they'd been the night he hit me. What could I do? I half expected to hear Fatima's voice breathing words of wisdom, advising me what to say, but there was nothing.

"All right," I said finally. "I'll go."

Almost immediately, I found myself fretting about Fatima. I don't know why, but the thought popped into my head that she might live near Cable Street. The idea scared me. I felt embarrassed, too. I didn't want her to watch me march past with hundreds of stone-faced Fascists. Of course, I'd never seen Fatima's eyes but I imagined how sad and disappointed they would look to see me in such company. If only I could send my thoughts back to her, warn her about Dad's nasty surprise for the Muslims of East London.

I concentrated hard:

Fatima, this is Georgie. Can you hear me? Stay away from Cable Street. The Fascists are planning to march there again.

Nothing.

Fatima, please, you've got to listen to me. They want to frighten you. They want to drive you away.

I tried again and again, but there was no response. It seemed as if I was sending radio signals to a dead planet. Fatima sent nothing back, nor did any of the other children whose voices I'd been hearing.

I suddenly felt abandoned by them, as if they'd deliberately tuned me out. It seemed I was no longer part of their network.

MELISSA

Mr Millington was always late for our History lessons. He'd arrive red-faced and sweaty, whatever the weather, with his shirt untucked, carrying a coffee he'd brought from the staff room in a "World's Greatest Teacher" mug. I'd told him once that he must have paid for it himself because none of us kids would have given it to him as a present. But that was the old me. I realise now that those kinds of put-downs are hurtful and unhelpful, even though Mr Millington was a pig and sort of deserved them. Anyway, he was late, which meant I had at least five minutes to talk to the class about Fatima.

Without a teacher there, everyone was messing around. Artsem and Mikhail were shouting in Russian and flicking bits of wet paper at the windows. Kele was spinning his battered old basketball on one finger. Some of the girls were practising this dumb dance they wanted to do in assembly; they always wanted to do a dance in assembly.

I needed to get everyone's attention, so I just covered my ears with my hands and screamed really loudly. Straightaway the room went silent. Everyone stared at me, waiting to see what I would do next. I knew people had seen a big change in me recently, but they still shut up and took notice whenever I screamed at them.

"Thank you," I said, smiling my sweetest smile. "Sorry about that."

One of Kele's eyebrows arched upwards as though it was on a string yanked by a puppeteer.

"That was loud, Melissa," he said.

"Yeah, sorry, but what it is, is that I need to aks you all a big favour."

Leona and Kodi started smirking. They hid their pouty little mouths behind their hands when I glared at them.

"There's this man," I said, "like a really bad man. He's a Fascist and he's coming with a lot of other Fascists to march through Tower Hamlets tomorrow. He wants to frighten everyone – kids like me and all of you who have different coloured skin, or religions, or whatever. He wants us to leave this country and go somewhere else, even if we was born here. I have this friend called Fatima and she says we've got to join together and stop him."

Simone smiled, but not a friendly smile.

"Why don't you just scream at him, Melissa, until he goes away?"

I could feel myself getting stressed and I dug my fingernails into the palms of my hands.

"I ain't never seen you with no one called Fatima," Kodi added, her eyes narrowing.

"Look, I really need your help. Fatima says if we all meet at this place called Cable Street, we might be able to stop him. She says sometimes you just have to stand up for yourself. It's like not letting bullies push you around. And that's what these fascists are, they're bullies."

"I can't help you," Leona said. "I've got to go shopping with my mum and my sister, then we're going McDonalds."

This wasn't working out how I'd imagined. I scanned their faces to see if I was getting through to any of them.

"So will there be like a massive ruck?" Mikhail asked. "You're going to need a lot of kids if you're planning to fight against grown-ups."

"You're going to need guns too, man," his mate Artsem said. "AK 47s!"

Artsem was small and skinny with mousy brown hair. I felt like I could have crushed his tiny skull between my finger and thumb.

Suddenly I heard Fatima's soothing voice whispering to me.

If enough of us come, they'll turn back. We don't need to bring weapons, just ourselves.

I cleared my throat.

"We won't need guns, Artsem. If enough of us show up tomorrow, we can block off Cable Street and they won't be able to get through."

Leona, Kodi and Simone started tittering.

"At the moment, Melissa," Leona said, "it's just you who's going. But I suppose you could always block the street on your own."

I looked down at my huge hands.

"You calling me fat?" I asked quietly.

Leona blinked.

"I know I'm fat, but I'd prefer it if you called me that word Miss de Souza looked up. What was it? *Statuesque* – yeah, like a big, beautiful statue."

Leona gave me something close to a proper smile this time.

"OK, Melissa, you're a big beautiful statue, but I still can't see anyone's going to go with you tomorrow."

"Actually, I'll be going," said a voice from over by the store cupboard.

I just stared at Kele. He was holding his basketball on one hip and jutting out his chin.

"Yeah, I figure the Nigerians should be represented there, innit Melissa?"

I couldn't speak, I felt my eyes getting watery. I just nodded, and as I did, the tears threatened to flow down my cheeks.

"Thank you, Kel," I said.

That's when Mr Millington arrived. He tried to nudge the door open with his shoulder, but it bounced back off a chair wedged behind it and jolted his coffee mug. Leona and her girlfriends laughed. Mr Millington glowered at them, then stared angrily at the watery brown stains on his light grey trousers and the small puddle that was spreading across the carpet between his feet.

"Don't just stand there gawping, Kele. Put that blessed ball down and get a cloth," he snapped.

Once Mr Millington had made a space for his half-empty mug on the desk, it seemed to occur to him that he hadn't walked in on the usual riot in our classroom.

"Thank you for waiting so, er, patiently," he said. "What have you been talking about? Not History, I assume."

He grinned, but to himself, not to us.

Kele stopped scrubbing the carpet and looked up at him.

"We were talking about Cable Street, sir."

Mr Millington frowned.

"What, the Battle of Cable Street? Seriously?"

Artsem and Mikhail glanced at each other. Presumably they had visions of machine guns and tanks in their heads again.

I was confused. I'd understood that Fatima only spoke to other children. I couldn't imagine her sending out her thought-waves to someone like Mr Millington.

"What do you mean by the *Battle* of Cable Street?" I asked him.

"It was some time in the 1930s – 1936, I think. The Fascists tried to march through the East End to intimidate the Jews who lived there. But they were stopped by a big army of local people. If you look at the photographs, you can see many of the locals were carrying banners that said, 'They shall not pass'. And, amazingly, the Fascists were turned back. If you go to Cable Street now, there's a big mural — you know, a painting on a wall that shows it all. It's really rather good."

"So it's happened already?" Artsem said, looking disappointed. "The Fascists aren't going to try it again? Like tomorrow?"

Mr Millington shook his head. It was as bald as Kele's basketball.

"No. No way. They'd never get permission. It would be really threatening to the local people who live there now, because most of them are Muslims from Bangladesh. The Fascists would never be allowed to march down Cable Street again."

I was almost too scared to glance across at Kele. Surely he wouldn't come with me now. And since everyone else respected him, they wouldn't come along either. But when I finally did catch Kele's eye, he just shrugged his shoulders and gave me this look that said, "What does that idiot Mr Millington know about anything?"

"So you'll be there?" I mouthed at him.

"Yeah," he mouthed back. "Of course."

GEORGE

When Dad and I arrived at the City end of Cable Street, hundreds of his supporters were already milling around under the railway arches. Dad was wearing a dark suit and a light brown cashmere overcoat: Mr Respectable. But many of his followers looked like most people's idea of thugs in their green bomber jackets and laced-up boots. Brian, Dad's super-sized bodyguard, was there to meet our taxi.

"All right, George?" He nodded at Dad and gave me a cold look as if I was an insect that had landed on him. I'd known Brian for as long as I could remember and he'd never looked at me that way before. He seemed almost disgusted by me.

"All right, Georgie boy?" he said finally. "How are you feeling today? Don't want any more soppy behaviour from you, do we?"

Dad frowned at him.

"Shut it, Brian, will you? Georgie's fine. Never better."

"I was just. . ." Brian's deep bass voice trailed off.

"Like I said, just shut it," Dad repeated.

I saw a sign high on a wall that read 'Cable Street, E1', but there didn't seem to be any homes or even any people at this end of it. Above our heads, a train from the Docklands Light Railway clattered past. We began to march away from the City of London with all its wealth towards the poverty of the East End. I tried to count the bodies pressing around me but soon gave up. There must have been at least five hundred of us walking in the footsteps of Oswald Mosley and his Blackshirts. Usually at Dad's rallies there were songs and chants, but today we were silent apart from the tramping of boots. Dad had predicted it wouldn't take long for the police to get wind of our illegal gathering and start arriving in their vans and squad cars. Maybe they'd even send out a helicopter and shout at us through loudhailers to turn back. But by then it would be too late. George Smith and his fascist followers would have marched down Cable Street in a show of strength. George Smith would have done what Oswald Mosley and his Blackshirts failed to do.

I couldn't see above the heads of the marchers in front of me and, being short, neither could Dad. I assumed that once we'd gone a bit further, Dad would want to lead the march, but for the moment he seemed happy to be in amongst his people. Cable Street is about a mile long and I guessed we'd need fifteen minutes or so to walk the whole length of it. I'd given myself over to the rhythm of our marching, when suddenly an electric charge of tension passed through our ranks and the

row of people in front of me stopped dead.
Dad and I bumped into their backs and came to
a halt; then the people behind us did the same
until we were all jammed up close.

"What's going on?" Dad called out.

He sounded confident, still in control.

It was Mart's voice that carried back to him
over the rows of heads.

"Boss, I think you should come up here and
see this."

Dad took hold of my sleeve and began
pushing his way to the front of our lines.
It wasn't easy and our progress was slow.

"Is it the Old Bill?" Dad shouted.

I knew the one thing that had bothered him
all along was that the police would turn up too
quickly and spoil his big moment.

"No," Mart called back. "There's no sign of
them."

Finally the bodies in front of us had parted
enough for me to see what lay ahead. A cold
wind was whipping our faces, but suddenly
I felt my cheeks flush. My whole body tingled.

We'd reached the first part of the St George's housing estate, its grey tower blocks looming over the right side of the street. It was home to many of the Muslims who Dad planned to terrorise. When I'd looked at the estate on a map, I'd half imagined that this was where Fatima lived. Now, spilling out from the far end of it and onto the road was a massive crowd. I couldn't guess their number, but it was many more than we had brought to Cable Street. This crowd was huge and it was blocking our way.

From a pocket in his quilted coat, Brian had produced the small pair of binoculars he took with him when he went to the races. When I was younger he'd let me play with them. But he wasn't in the mood for fun and games now. As he passed the binoculars to my dad, Brian wore the look of an angry and confused gorilla.

"You ain't gonna believe this, George," he said. "But it's kids. Must be a thousand of 'em."

Dad squinted through the binoculars.

"Well I'll be. . ." he muttered.

"What do you want to do, boss?" Brian asked him.

I sensed that about five hundred members of the British Fascist Party were extremely interested in the answer to that question.

Finally Dad let out a weird laugh.

"What do I want to do, Brian? I want to march right up to them and tell them to go and play somewhere else. And if they don't agree to that, I'm going to march right over them. We've come too far to be stopped by a bunch of children."

He flashed an angry look in my direction. For a second I wondered if he'd thought that this was somehow my doing. Then he shouted hoarsely at his followers as if they were a gang of football hooligans about to charge at rival fans. He might have been wearing a smart suit but suddenly he looked far from respectable. The veins stood out in his neck and his eyes looked like they might pop out of their sockets.

"Come on. . !" he shouted, and it sounded like a war cry.

Then he started jogging towards them. We all did. All five hundred of us.

MELISSA

I won't say I wasn't scared, because I was, especially when the Fascists started running towards us. But I felt strong. Kele was on one side of me and – the most amazing thing – Fatima was on the other. She held onto my arm because, as everyone knows now, she's blind and she needs someone to guide her when she goes outside. But you sort of forget that she can't see because she's so calm and intelligent and powerful. That's why so many people joined her in Cable Street that day.

I couldn't believe how many had come. We filled up the road from one side to the other and when I looked behind me, there was this huge sea of faces all lined up close together. It was as if the entire crowd at a pop concert in a big stadium had been dropped down into this one narrow street. No way was anyone going to get through us. And that's what it said on this huge banner some of the children were carrying: 'They Shall Not Pass'.

I squeezed Fatima's hand.

"You always said we'd meet up when the time was right. So can you talk to all these kids in your head?"

Fatima laughed, and it was a lovely sound like a musical instrument might make.

"No, Melissa. Most of these children have come because they listened to people like you. The word has spread, and not just by thought-waves."

It was really nice of Fatima to praise me like that. The truth was that of all the kids in my class, only Kele and the two Russian boys had come. But I suppose that was a start, and look where it had finished – with maybe a thousand of us here in Cable Street.

As the Fascists got closer and closer we all went quiet. They were running together in a rhythm, like they thought they were American marines or something. When we'd come out of the housing estate and filled up the road, we'd been buzzing like bees flying out of a hive. Now you couldn't hear anything apart from kids shuffling nervously from one foot to the other and the sound of the Fascists' boots.

When they were a few metres away from what Fatima called our "human barricade", they just stopped. Some of them looked big and proper-hard but I think they couldn't work out whether to hit us or laugh at us. We were only kids, after all.

Then Fatima let go of me and took one step forward. It was almost funny to try and guess what the Fascists made of her – this small, skinny, blind girl in a headscarf. Of course, any one of them could have picked her up like a doll and smashed her until she lay still on the ground. But they didn't, they just stared at her.

Finally she spoke out loud. It was her usual greeting, but this time it was in her actual voice.

"My name is Fatima. I know that you can hear me."

GEORGIE

The moment she said her name, Dad swung round and looked at me. He was out of breath from running and couldn't speak at first. Mind you, what we saw in Cable Street that day was enough to leave anyone speechless. We'd spotted this huge crowd of kids from a long way off. But now we were only a few metres away from them, they appeared to be led by a frail girl in a headscarf with sightless eyes. Like my dad, she seemed to have brought a bodyguard or two along with her as well as the hundreds of children who now blocked our way. The most striking of them was this giant black girl who glared at us, daring anyone to make a move towards her smaller friend.

Dad took a few more seconds to compose himself, then he flashed his most winning smile at Fatima and the throng of children behind her.

"Good morning to you, Fatima, darling. It's lovely to meet you, but you're giving me and my friends here a bit of a problem. And I'd like to sort it out as quickly as possible."

"You are George Smith, the fascist?"

Dad laughed.

"I've been called a lot worse than that, but yes, I am George Smith, the fascist. Now I really need you and your friends to run along and play somewhere else."

Fatima rose up to her full height.

"Do not talk down to us, Mr Smith. We know why you're here. You want to march along Cable Street. You want to frighten people and tell them they're not welcome in this country. But as our banner says, you shall not pass."

A shadow seemed to move across Dad's features.

"Don't be silly, young lady. You won't be able to stop my boys if I unleash them. At the moment they're being very patient. But if I ask them to run at you, I promise they'll do it. And a lot of you will get very badly hurt."

He raised his voice to address all the children who were blocking the street.

"Is that what you lot want? Do you want to get hurt? Or do you want to just walk away from here and get on with your lives?"

A tall, long-limbed black boy who looked like a basketball player shouted back at my dad.

"We ain't going nowhere, Smith. Look at the size of this crowd. You won't be marching through us today. There's too many of us. It ain't going to happen."

I could see that Dad was starting to lose it and I feared what would happen next.

"All right kids," he said. "You asked for it. . ."

He lifted his right arm like an old-time

general about to command his troops to advance, but before any words could pass his lips, Fatima spoke again.

"Wait! Why don't you ask your son what he thinks before you charge at us."

Dad let his arm drop to his side. I felt that everyone was suddenly staring at me. Then Fatima's voice was in my head, calm and soothing.

Don't be afraid, Georgie. You know what you must do. It's time to choose which side you're on. Come across. Come and join us.

I looked at my dad and then at Fatima. She had spread out her arms in a beckoning gesture. We were only a few metres apart but I knew if I started walking towards her, it would be the most important journey I'd ever make. On one side of this no-man's-land was my dad who I still loved despite everything. On the other was a new world that I found I could no longer hate.

Come, Georgie. It's time to do what's right.

And so I walked.

I don't know how many steps it took, but it felt as if I was moving through a slow-motion dream. And then I was there. I'd crossed over. I was standing next to Fatima, looking back at the Fascists and my dad.

"Georgie, what the hell are you doing? Come back here now!" he roared.

I shook my head

"I'm tired of your hatred and your fear of anything different, Dad. And d'you know what, all this stuff about keeping the white race pure – it's history. You're living in the past. When you look at us, you're looking at the future. These kids are the future of our country, whatever their colour or religion. And I'm standing with them now, whether you like it or not."

My dad scanned the faces of the children around me – white, brown, black, pretty much every shade of skin there is to be found. Then he fixed me again with those famous blue eyes.

"That was quite a speech, Georgie boy.

Maybe you should think of going into politics."

I looked at his bodyguards, Brian, Mart and Tony. Their eyes were all on Dad, waiting for him to tell them what to do. I could hear the wail of police sirens now, coming closer to Cable Street. No doubt the press photographers would find their way here soon.

"It's up to you, Dad," I shouted. "You can try and fight your way through if you like, but we won't just lie down and let you walk all over us. And that won't look good on the TV or in the newspapers – a bunch of fascists wading into a crowd of kids."

Brian was scowling at me from across the divide. I could see he was weary of waiting for something to happen. And many of the other Fascists were getting agitated and muttering amongst themselves.

"Come on, boss, make a decision," he boomed. "What are we going to do?"

My Dad stared at Brian as though he no longer recognised him. Then he looked one last time at me. His face was pale and strained, and he suddenly seemed much older. When he finally spoke, his voice was barely audible.

"OK, Georgie, I know when I'm beaten. You and your new mates have won this battle. I'm going home."

For a second I could hear cries of anger and confusion from some of the Fascists close by him. But they were soon drowned out by an enormous cheer from behind me. It washed over us all like the noise of a football crowd when a crucial goal has been scored, but it kept on coming. And then I realised why. The Fascists were retreating, in small groups at first. But soon, like a receding tide, they all began trudging back the way they had come. In amongst them was my dad, fists thrust deep into his pockets, his shoulders hunched. Some of the Fascists jostled him and swore at him. They jabbed their fingers in my direction. No doubt they blamed him for raising a son like me – a boy who had grown up to betray them all.

It suddenly struck me that my dad might never speak to me again, and the thought crushed the life out of me. My lungs seemed to stop working properly. I found myself panting for air.

That's when the first rock hit me. It didn't even hurt, it just bounced off my shoulder. Then I felt the children who were pressing closely around me sway backwards. Stones, rocks, even bits of brick, were suddenly raining down on us. A breakaway group of Fascists, led by Brian, Dad's bodyguard, had found a builders' skip full of rubble and were lobbing chunks of it in our direction.

"You asked for this!" Brian shouted, his fat face throbbing with hate. I realised with a shiver that he was glaring directly at me.

"This is what you muppets wanted. So this is what you're going to get."

As more stones and lumps of rubble fell, panic spread amongst the children and gaps started opening in our human barricade. I saw two girls fall clutching their heads. They got to their feet again but they were screaming and there was blood too.

"We've got to stand firm," I cried. "Once the police get here, they'll give up. We've just got to hold for a few more minutes."

A convoy of police cars and vans was speeding towards us from the City end of Cable Street but Brian and the fifty or so remaining Fascists continued to hurl their makeshift weapons of bricks and stones.

"Stand firm, all of you!" I shouted again. "We mustn't let them pass."

But suddenly the big black girl who'd been standing with Fatima let out a terrifying shriek as though she herself had been hit. Other children gasped.

A rock, bigger than a man's fist, had struck Fatima on the side of the head. She fell like a small fluttering bird that had dropped out of the sky, then lay motionless in the middle of Cable Street.

Almost at once, I was aware of a strange vibration in the air, a humming sound, as hundreds of worried voices called her name telepathically. Nothing came back from her. She lay totally still, her face obscured by her headscarf.

Finally, the first police vans pulled up with a screech of their tyres. Dozens of officers jumped out and began wrestling with the last of the Fascists. I saw Brian lumbering off across some scrubland. They hadn't breached our lines. We had held firm. But at what cost?

Three paramedics in fluorescent yellow uniforms pushed through the crush of anxious children to Fatima's crumpled body. I suddenly felt as though my head had been drained of blood, that I too might drop down onto the ground that Fatima had done so much to defend. Cable Street had seen another famous victory, but all I could think about was that she was badly injured, or worse.

The paramedics lifted her onto a stretcher then carried her to their yellow and green London ambulance. They moved slowly and solemnly. Their grim faces left little doubt in my mind: Fatima was dead.

The crowd of children pressed close to the doors of the vehicle as they clunked shut. Many of them were crying, including the big black girl whose whole body shuddered as she sobbed.

"I was meant to protect her," she howled. "It was me that was meant to look after her."

I saw a skinny, dazed-looking Asian boy I hadn't noticed before. Suddenly, he began to hammer with his fists on the side of the ambulance. His voice was shrill and full of pain.

"I'm her brother. You've got to let me go with her. You've got to let me in."

It seemed the ambulance crew were ignoring him. The driver had switched on the flashing blue lights and was starting to pull away. But then one of the doors swung open and Fatima's brother clambered inside.

Everyone stepped back as the ambulance sped off. All I could hear now was children weeping and the siren's desperate wail. From

Fatima, there was nothing.

Bitterness began to bubble up inside me like poison. Fatima's death was my dad's fault. He might as well have thrown the rock himself. If he hadn't brought his fascist thugs to Cable Street, she would still be alive. He'd come here dressed in his smart suit and coat, but he was a thug just like the rest of them. I loathed him, despised everything he believed in. I no longer cared if we never spoke again.

And then I heard Fatima's voice inside my head once more.

At first it was so soft I thought I must be imagining it. Suddenly there was no room inside me for anything but joy.

You're being too hard, Georgie. It's time to forgive now. Time to make things right.

You're alive? I bounced the thought right back in her direction.

I'm bruised and I feel dazed, but I'm sure I will be fine.

"She's alive." I whispered. Then I started to shout it until my lungs felt close to bursting.

"She's alive! Fatima's alive! She's going to be all right!"

My words were taken up by the children who'd been milling around in shock on Cable Street. They radiated further, like ripples on the surface of the Thames, stretching out across London and beyond. I became aware of thousands of minds all linked together; all thinking the same thought; all rejoicing as one.

She's alive! Fatima is alive!

We had won and Fatima was alive. But she could so easily have been killed – an innocent girl murdered by extremists. Despite my elation, the anger I felt for my dad began to flare again.

Of course, Fatima would have none of it. And as she spoke, I felt my rage dying down, at least for now.

Georgie, I've told you already, it's time to forgive! We have touched many hearts this day and I believe your father too will change. You have sown a seed in his mind, Georgie. Remember, flowers can grow in stony places.

ABOUT THE STORY

People have asked what drew me to the Battle of Cable Street as a subject for my latest book. Well firstly, it's not as widely-known as it should be, even though it's a great example of people from different backgrounds coming together to fight racism. Also, although I'm not Jewish, it feels personal to me.

My grandma grew up in a little terraced house off Cable Street in London's East End. The world she knew was poor and grimy and noisy, but she loved it. And for her it was made richer by the Jewish people who lived around her. She loved their exotic foods and the sights and sounds of their markets. Most of all she loved her best friend, Edie Cohen, who lived a few doors away and who happened to be a Jew.

My grandma's family had lived in the East End for as many generations as anyone could remember, and she was fiercely proud of it. She grew up alongside children who had come from all over the world: Irish, Italians, Chinese and Indians, as well as Jews from Russia, Poland and Romania. To men like the British fascist leader Sir Oswald Mosley, these children were unwelcome.

To my grandma they were East Enders, just like her, who were simply trying to make a life.

As for me, I grew up with three adopted brothers: one black, one white, one brown. Like all brothers, we fought at times but we always stuck up for each other. And we loved each other as much as any of the so-called blood brothers we knew. People say that blood is thicker than water. I don't believe that.

My family background has had a big influence on my attitudes to the multicultural country we live in, as well as the kind of stories I want to write. Above all, I believe in the idea that we're all in it together, whatever the colour of our skin.

**Read on for an exclusive preview
of the first chapter of**

OMAR

When I first heard his voice, late that autumn night, my nerves were already messed up. Whitechapel High Street, eleven o'clock. A drunken old tramp had just lurched across the pavement towards me like a wild-eyed zombie. There was even a ghostly mist in the damp East London air. It felt as if I was walking through the set of a cheap horror film.

My name is Jack. I know that you can hear me. Please be afraid!

Someone's idea of a joke - nothing to get freaked out about. That's what I told myself. Remember, I've been hearing voices all my life, starting with my sister Fatima's. She has always been able to read my mind, share her thoughts with me, even when we are far apart. But this wasn't a child's voice or even a young person's.

It was deep and strange, and 'Jack' was using Fatima's trademark greeting.

I said, I know that you can hear me, Omar.

I actually swung around to check if he was behind me, even though I knew this was a 'thought-voice'. When you're telepathic you get used to people dropping into your brain for a chat. They're usually friendly. You hardly ever feel threatened by them.

I began walking faster, cursing my father and his forgetfulness. It was his fault that I was out on the streets at all. How many times had he left his glasses at home? And how often had I been called to bring them to our uncle's restaurant so my father could see well enough to sort out the evening's takings?

You seem afraid, Omar, and I like that. You should be scared of me.

I decided to ignore him and his weird, mocking voice. But it's not easy to block people's thoughts. Jack knew that I could hear him. If you try to screen out a thought-voice, it's like not picking up the phone when someone knows you're at home.

I won't be ignored, Omar. That's one thing I cannot stand. I've been around a long time. And people take notice of me.

I'd reached the neon-lit street in Bangla Town where my uncle's restaurant jostled for business alongside all the others. At last I could start to relax. My father wasn't telepathic, nor was my mother or my big brother Sadiq. But they knew about me and Fatima and what my father called our "gift". I would tell my father about the creepy voice I'd been hearing and ask if I could wait to walk home with him.

Of course, it's your sister I'm most interested in, Omar. I've never liked goodness. It's always brought out the worst in me.

I clenched my jaw, my fists. No one threatened my sister - I'd merk them if they dared. But suddenly, I was flying through the foggy night, sent sprawling by a black bin-liner full of rubbish.

I rubbed the pavement grit off the palms of my hands. The fall had ripped the cloth of my trousers and my left knee was grazed. As I got up, I glanced into a shadowy alley that ran down the side of an off-licence. What I saw there made me shiver. Looming out of the darkness was a tall figure. I could not make out his features but he was beckoning me towards him with long, bony fingers.

"Come and help me, there's a good boy. I just need a bit of change if you've got any on yer."

I laughed out loud. It was just another old tramp begging for money. I felt relieved, as well as stupid for letting myself get so worked up. That's when I heard Jack's voice again.

Look further down, Omar, past the old fool and the dustbins. It's dark isn't it, but can you see me? I won't stay in the shadows forever, Omar. This is just the beginning. Even I don't know where it will end. . .

For a second, I felt too frozen to move. I was afraid for myself and scared for the old tramp too.

"Get out of there, you're in danger!" I screamed. Then, without looking back, I ran.

Joe Layburn has spent most of his life in
East London. His dad thought it would be
fantastic for Joe and his three brothers to grow up
surrounded by the fresh air and green fields
of the country but Joe missed London and
moved back as soon as he could.

Joe was a TV reporter and journalist for
15 years before becoming a teacher.
He has always loved writing stories and the
modern and historical East End is
a big inspiration for him.

Joe lives in East London with his wife
Marianne and three sons, Richie, Charlie and Hal.
Joe and his sons are season-ticket holders at
West Ham football club. His other book
for Frances Lincoln is *Ghostscape*.